PUFFIN BOOKS
Published by the Penguin Group: London, New York, Australia,
Canada, India, Ireland, New Zealand and South Africa
Penguin Books Ltd, Registered Offices: 80 Strand, London WC2R 0RL, England

puffinbooks.com

First published 2010
001
Characters and artwork are the original creation of Tove Jansson
Text and illustrations copyright © Moomin Characters™, 2010
Made and printed in China
ISBN: 978-0-141-37500-7

MOOMIN
and the
Birthday Button

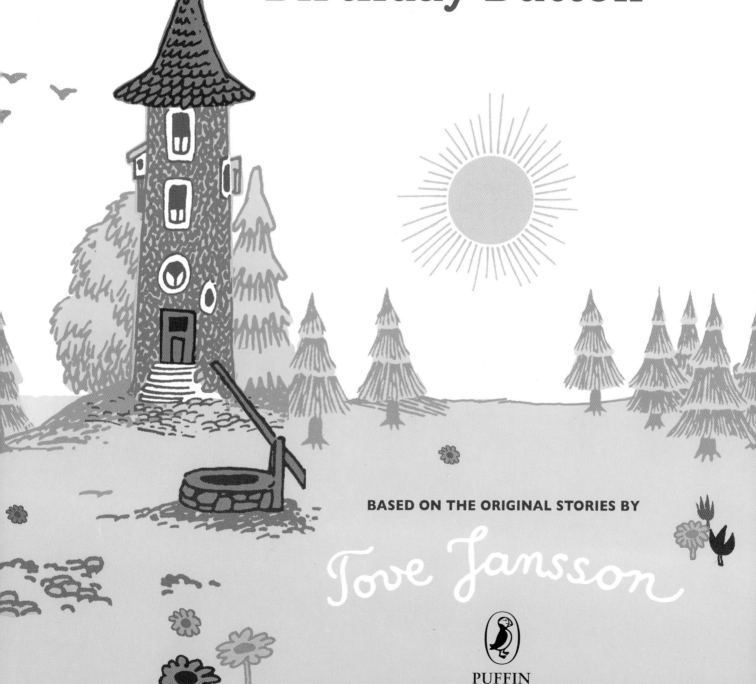

BASED ON THE ORIGINAL STORIES BY

Tove Jansson

PUFFIN

The moon faded, the sun rose, and morning came to Moominvalley. Snug in his bed in the Moominhouse, Moomintroll woke up.

He yawned **once**, he stretched **twice**, and then he remembered . . .

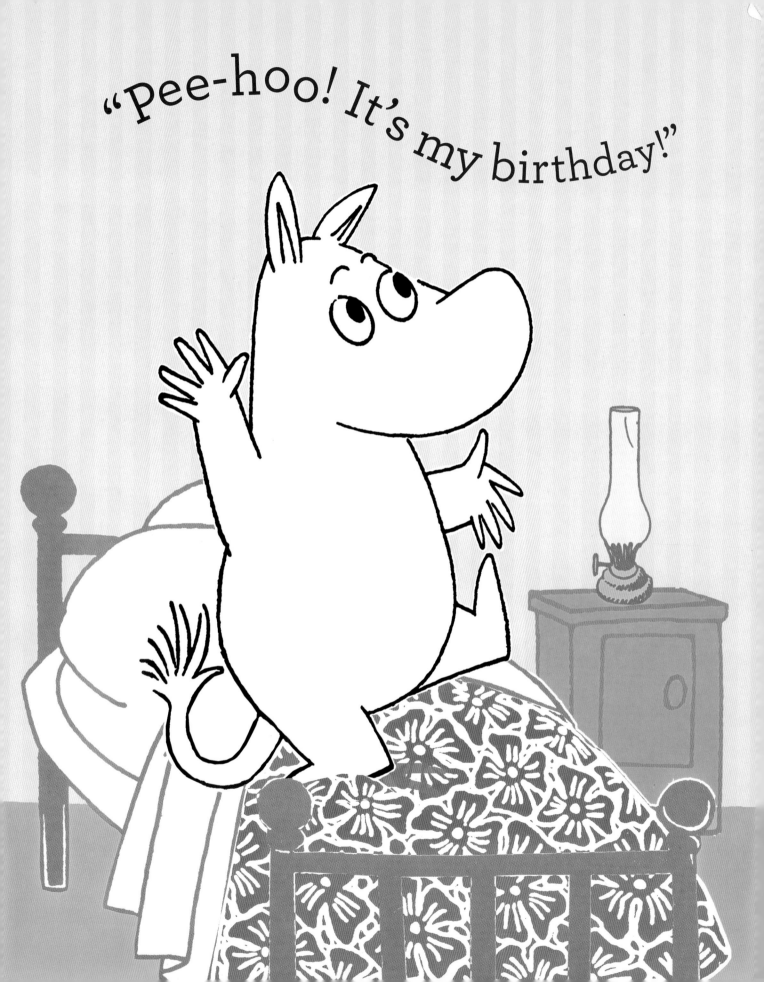

Downstairs, Moominmamma and Moominpappa were having breakfast. They called out,

"Happy Birthday, Moomintroll!"

There was a card from Moominpappa with a birthday poem he'd written, and a beautiful gold button from Moominmamma for his collection.

"Oh, it's so perfect and shiny," said Moomin, "I'm going to show Snufkin straightaway."

Snufkin was down by the river. He was
busy making something out of wood.
Moomin called out,
    "Snufkin, look what I've got!"

But Snufkin didn't even look up.
"I'll look later," he mumbled.
"I'm really terribly busy right now."

Moomintroll was surprised.
"I'll go and show Snorkmaiden instead,"
he thought. "*She* won't be too busy."

On his way to find Snorkmaiden, he bumped into Sniff who seemed to be searching for something.

"Hello, Sniff," said Moomin. "Look what I've got!"

But Sniff didn't look up either!

"Sorry, Moomintroll," he said. "Too busy, can't stop."

"How odd that Sniff is too busy, too," thought Moomin. "But I know Snorkmaiden will like my button." And he hurried on his way.

Snorkmaiden was at the beach collecting shells.
She seemed to be having a lot of fun with Little My,
who was draping herself with seaweed.

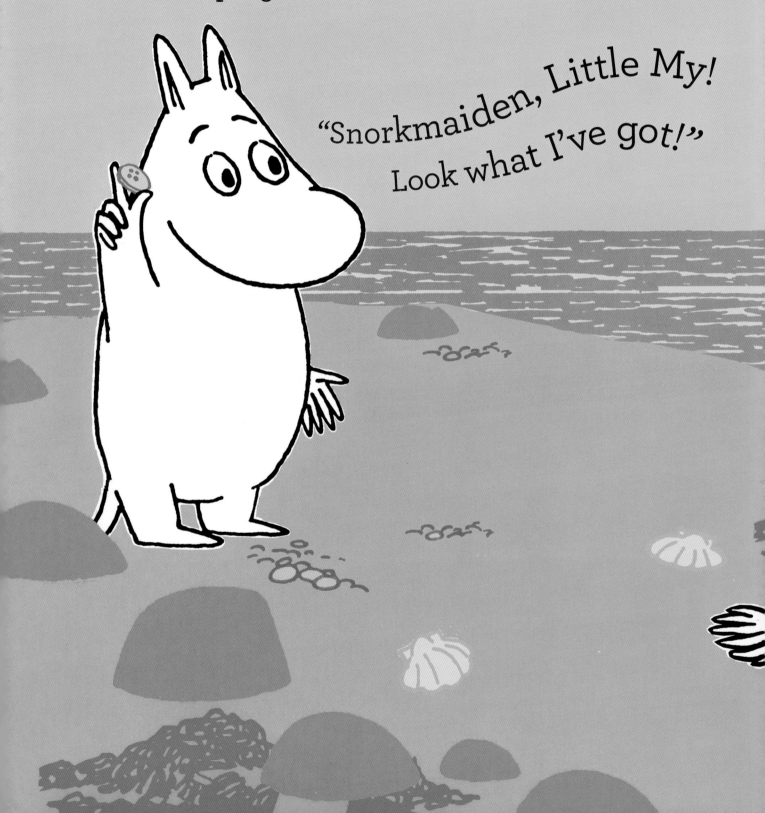

"Snorkmaiden, Little My!
Look what I've got!"

But Snorkmaiden didn't answer. She just went on looking for shells.

Little My danced about and shouted, "We're very busy, Moomintroll. Don't disturb us!"

Moomin couldn't believe his ears. "Nobody wants to see my new button," he thought. "And nobody has even said 'Happy Birthday'!"

He stamped back through the woods and by the time he reached home he was nearly in tears.

When Moominmamma saw Moomintroll she knew at once that something was wrong.

"Nobody cares about my new button or my birthday," sniffed Moomin. "They're all too busy. Even Snorkmaiden!"

"Don't be sad," said Moominmamma.
"I'm sure they didn't mean to be unkind.

Come on – let's get things ready for your birthday tea."

Moomin cheered up a little as he watched Moominmamma decorate his birthday cake. But he was still cross.

"They're probably too busy to come," he said. "I don't even care!" But he did, really.

Then, all of a sudden, he heard voices calling him.

"Moomintroll, come outside! Come and look what we've got!"

Moomintroll rushed to the door and there were all his friends . . .

Snorkmaiden, Sniff, Little My and Snufkin!

Sniff was holding a present, which was very badly wrapped in seaweed!
  "This is for you," he said.
"From all of us."

Moomin could have burst with happiness. They hadn't forgotten his birthday after all!

He unwrapped the present and inside was a beautiful wooden treasure chest that was decorated with pebbles and shells.

"Snufkin made it, and I chose the shells," said Snorkmaiden.

"The pebbles are my very favourite ones that I've ever found," said Sniff. "I nearly kept them for myself."

"And I wrapped it!" said Little My.

The sun set, the moon rose and night fell over Moominvalley.

Moomintroll and his friends sang birthday songs and

danced, until they were all tired out and ready for bed.

"Night night, my little Moomintroll," said Moominmamma.

"Night night, Mamma," said Moomin.

But before he closed his eyes, Moomin had one last peep at the shiny new button glinting in his very special treasure chest.

"Happy Birthday, Moomintroll," he whispered to himself, and he drifted off to sleep.